THE LOST DINOSAUR BONE

BY MERCER MAYER

To Matilda Skiles,
Welcome to the World.
Glad You're Here!

⛬ HarperFestival®

A Division of HarperCollins*Publishers*

HarperCollins®, ⛬®, and HarperFestival® are trademarks of HarperCollins Publishers.
Copyright © 2007 Mercer Mayer. All rights reserved. LITTLE CRITTER, MERCER MAYER'S LITTLE CRITTER and
MERCER MAYER'S LITTLE CRITTER and logo are registered trademarks of Orchard House Licensing Company. All rights reserved.
No part of this book may be used or reproduced in any manner whatsoever without written permission
except in the case of brief quotations embodied in critical articles and reviews. Printed in the United States of America.
For information address HarperCollins Children's Books, a division of HarperCollins Publishers, 1350 Avenue of the Americas, New York, NY 10019
Library of Congress catalog card number: 2006939823
A Big Tuna Trading Company, LLC/J. R. Sansevere Book
www.harpercollinschildrens.com   www.littlecritter.com
1 2 3 4 5 6 7 8 9 10
❖
First Edition

Our class went on a field trip to the Museum of Natural History. I couldn't wait to see the dinosaurs. When I grow up, I'm going to be a dinosaur hunter.

But when we got to the museum, the dinosaur exhibit was closed.

So, we had to see the butterflies instead. The butterflies were fun, but I really wished we could see the dinosaurs.

Next, we went to the Rain Forest. There were lots
of trees with monkeys in them.

"Oooh! Oooh!" I said to the monkeys.

A guard came running over to see the monkeys, too, so I asked him about the dinosaurs. I found out that the exhibit was closed because a Triceratops bone was missing!

In the Hall of Gems and Minerals it was very dark, so we had to wear miner hats with lights on them. Tiger went looking for diamonds, but I was busy looking for the missing dinosaur bone. No luck!

After that, we went to the Planetarium, where the ceiling turned into a sky filled with stars.

We found out that the planet Mars is covered with dust and that the planet Saturn has rings around it.

I kept my eye out for the dinosaur bone, but I didn't see it.

On our way to see a meteorite, I asked Miss Kitty if I
could get a drink of water.

When I found the fountain, I also found something
else—the dinosaur exhibit! It had a big sign saying
EXHIBIT CLOSED.

I went closer and saw a Tyrannosaurus rex. It was heading right for me!

I ran away as fast as I could . . .

. . . and found myself face-to-face with a Velociraptor. It had its mouth open wide so I could see all its sharp, pointy teeth.

The guard told me the exhibit was closed because of
the missing dinosaur bone.

"I know," I said. "I've been looking for it everywhere."

On my way out, I took a wrong turn. That's when I saw something long and white sticking out from under the Ankylosaurus skeleton. It was the missing dinosaur bone!

I ran back to tell the guard.
He didn't believe me at first . . .

. . . but when I
showed the bone to
him, he gave me this
big smile.

Then I told Miss Kitty, and the guard took our whole class to the special place where the scientists who study dinosaur bones work.

"Thank you for solving the mystery of the missing Triceratops bone," the scientists told me.

COMPSOGNATHUS
A VERY TINY
DINOSAUR

DIRT DAWG

The scientists took us on a tour of the dinosaur exhibit. They showed us a Stegosaurus skeleton they had found buried in a mountain.

"I'm going to be a dinosaur hunter when I grow up!" I said.

"You already are," answered the scientists.

You know what I'm going to do tomorrow?
Dig for dinosaur bones in my backyard!